Take Me to School With You!

by Sonali Fry
Illustrated by The Thompson Brothers

Based on the Scholastic book series
"Clifford The Big Red Dog"
by Norman Bridwell

SCHOLASTIC INC.

New York   Toronto   London   Auckland   Sydney
Mexico City   New Delhi   Hong Kong   Buenos Aires

Clifford had a wonderful summer with his best friend, Emily Elizabeth.

They went swimming.

They went camping.

They played games . . .

and they read books.

But summer was over, and it was time for Emily Elizabeth to go back to school. Clifford was very sad.

I wish she could take me to school with her.

"Don't worry, Clifford," said Emily Elizabeth. "I'll be home soon."

Clifford tried to keep busy.

"Maybe I'll play with my toys,"
he said to himself.
But he didn't feel like playing.

Then Clifford decided to take a nap.
But he tossed and turned.

Clifford couldn't even eat a doggy treat.
He missed Emily Elizabeth too much.

Then Clifford had an idea: What if Emily Elizabeth missed him, too?
Maybe she wanted to come home and play with him!

Clifford had to find out, so he ran toward the schoolhouse.

When he got there, Emily Elizabeth wasn't alone.
She was laughing and playing with her friends.

I guess she doesn't miss me after all.

"There you are!" said Cleo. "We've been looking all over for you!"

"I went to visit Emily Elizabeth, but she was busy playing with her friends. I guess she doesn't miss me," said Clifford sadly.

"Emily Elizabeth loves you," said T-Bone. "But she has to go to school."

"Come on, big guy," said Cleo. "Emily Elizabeth will be out of school soon. Let's play in the park until then."

So Clifford, T-Bone, and Cleo went to the park.

They played tug-of-war.

They jumped in leaf piles.

Clifford was having fun, but when the school bell rang, off he went!

When Clifford got to the schoolhouse,
Emily Elizabeth was walking out the door.

As soon as she saw Clifford, Emily Elizabeth
ran to him and gave him a big hug.
"Clifford! I missed you so-o-o-o much," she said.

Woof!

Clifford was happy. Now he and Emily Elizabeth
could play together the rest of the afternoon!

"Good-bye, Miss Carrington," said Emily Elizabeth as they left.

"Bye, Emily Elizabeth," replied Miss Carrington. "Don't forget to do your homework."

"I'll do it as soon as I get home!" said Emily Elizabeth.

Clifford's ears perked up. Wasn't Emily Elizabeth going to play with him?

Emily Elizabeth explained: "I really want to play, Clifford, but first I have to do my homework. I'll play with you as soon as I'm done."

Clifford remembered what T-Bone had said about Emily Elizabeth and how she had to go to school. So he waited patiently and hoped that she would soon be ready to play.

Finally, Emily Elizabeth was done with her homework!

"Okay, Clifford—I'm ready! But first, take a look at *this*," she said, showing him a piece of paper.

"Miss Carrington asked us to draw a picture of our favorite part of summer," explained Emily Elizabeth. "I drew a picture of us at the beach, because the best part for me was being with you!"

"I really wish I could take you to school with me. But this picture will be on my classroom wall. This way, I'll see you all the time!"

Clifford nuzzled close to Emily Elizabeth.

He realized that even though they couldn't be together all the time, Emily Elizabeth was still his best friend.